Marx
Hardy
Defoe Abbott Machiavelli Cooper Joyce Austen
Melville Montaigne Chesterton Emerson Hugo
Carroll Haggard Eliot Grimm
Stoker Christie Molière
Wilde Maupassant Byron Schiller
Garnett Engels Smith Kafka
Goethe Einstein Fitzgerald Hawthorne Hall
Cotton Dostoyevsky Willis
Baum Henry Kipling Doyle
Leslie Dumas Nietzsche
Flaubert Turgenev Balzac
Stockton Vatsyayana Crane
Burroughs Verne
Curtis Tocqueville Whitman Gogol Vinci
Homer Widger Tolstoy Busch
Darwin Thoreau
Potter Freud Zola Twain Scott
Kant Jowett Lawrence Plato Harte
Stevenson Dickens Hesse
Andersen Burton
London Descartes Cervantes Cooke
Poe Aristotle Wells Voltaire
Hale James Hastings
Bunner Shakespeare Irving
Richter Chambers
Doré da Shaw Benedict Alcott
Chekhov Pushkin
Dante Wodehouse Newton
Swift

 tredition®

tredition was established in 2006 by Sandra Latusseck and Soenke Schulz. Based in Hamburg, Germany, tredition offers publishing solutions to authors and publishing houses, combined with world-wide distribution of printed and digital book content. tredition is uniquely positioned to enable authors and publishing houses to create books on their own terms and without conventional manu-facturing risks.

For more information please visit: www.tredition.com

TREDITION CLASSICS

This book is part of the TREDITION CLASSICS series. The creators of this series are united by passion for literature and driven by the intention of making all public domain books available in printed format again - worldwide. Most TREDITION CLASSICS titles have been out of print and off the bookstore shelves for decades. At tredition we believe that a great book never goes out of style and that its value is eternal. Several mostly non-profit literature projects provide content to tredition. To support their good work, tredition donates a portion of the proceeds from each sold copy. As a reader of a TREDITION CLASSICS book, you support our mission to save many of the amazing works of world literature from oblivion. See all available books at www.tredition.com.

Project Gutenberg

The content for this book has been graciously provided by Project Gutenberg. Project Gutenberg is a non-profit organization founded by Michael Hart in 1971 at the University of Illinois. The mission of Project Gutenberg is simple: To encourage the creation and distribution of eBooks. Project Gutenberg is the first and largest collection of public domain eBooks.

A Strange Story

Volume 6

Baron Edward Bulwer Lytton Lytton

Imprint

This book is part of TREDITION CLASSICS

Author: Baron Edward Bulwer Lytton Lytton
Cover design: Buchgut, Berlin – Germany

Publisher: tredition GmbH, Hamburg - Germany
ISBN: 978-3-8424-3127-0

www.tredition.com
www.tredition.de

Copyright:
The content of this book is sourced from the public domain.

The intention of the TREDITION CLASSICS series is to make world literature in the public domain available in printed format. Literary enthusiasts and organizations, such as Project Gutenberg, worldwide have scanned and digitally edited the original texts. tredition has subsequently formatted and redesigned the content into a modern reading layout. Therefore, we cannot guarantee the exact reproduction of the original format of a particular historic edition. Please also note that no modifications have been made to the spelling, therefore it may differ from the orthography used today.

CHAPTER LIII.

There is an instance of the absorbing tyranny of every-day life which must have struck all such of my readers as have ever experienced one of those portents which are so at variance with every-day life, that the ordinary epithet bestowed on them is "supernatural."

And be my readers few or many, there will be no small proportion of them to whom once, at least, in the course of their existence, a something strange and eerie has occurred,—a something which perplexed and baffled rational conjecture, and struck on those chords which vibrate to superstition. It may have been only a dream unaccountably verified,—an undefinable presentiment or forewarning; but up from such slighter and vaguer tokens of the realm of marvel, up to the portents of ghostly apparitions or haunted chambers, I believe that the greater number of persons arrived at middle age, however instructed the class, however civilized the land, however sceptical the period, to which they belong, have either in themselves experienced, or heard recorded by intimate associates whose veracity they accept as indisputable in all ordinary transactions of life, phenomena which are not to be solved by the wit that mocks them, nor, perhaps, always and entirely, to the contentment of the reason or the philosophy that explains them away. Such phenomena, I say, are infinitely more numerous than would appear from the instances currently quoted and dismissed with a jest; for few of those who have witnessed them are disposed to own it, and they who only hear of them through others, however trustworthy, would not impugn their character for common-sense by professing a belief to which common-sense is a merciless persecutor. But he who reads my assertion in the quiet of his own room, will perhaps pause, ransack his memory, and find there, in some dark corner which he excludes from "the babbling and remorseless day," a pale recollection that proves the assertion not untrue.

And it is, I say, an instance of the absorbing tyranny of everyday life, that whenever some such startling incident disturbs its regular tenor of thought and occupation, that same every-day life hastens to bury in its sands the object which has troubled its surface; the more unaccountable, the more prodigious, has been the phenomenon which has scared and astounded us, the more, with involuntary effort, the mind seeks to rid itself of an enigma which might disease the reason that tries to solve it. We go about our mundane business with renewed avidity; we feel the necessity of proving to ourselves that we are still sober, practical men, and refuse to be unfitted for the world which we know, by unsolicited visitations from worlds into which every glimpse is soon lost amid shadows. And it amazes us to think how soon such incidents, though not actually forgotten, though they can be recalled — and recalled too vividly for health — at our will, are nevertheless thrust, as it were, out of the mind's sight as we cast into lumber-rooms the crutches and splints that remind us of a broken limb which has recovered its strength and tone. It is a felicitous peculiarity in our organization, which all members of my profession will have noticed, how soon, when a bodily pain is once passed, it becomes erased from the recollection, — how soon and how invariably the mind refuses to linger over and recall it. No man freed an hour before from a raging toothache, the rack of a neuralgia, seats himself in his armchair to recollect and ponder upon the anguish he has undergone. It is the same with certain afflictions of the mind, — not with those that strike on our affections, or blast our fortunes, overshadowing our whole future with a sense of loss; but where a trouble or calamity has been an accident, an episode in our wonted life, where it affects ourselves alone, where it is attended with a sense of shame and humiliation, where the pain of recalling it seems idle, and if indulged would almost madden us, — agonies of that kind we do not brood over as we do over the death or falsehood of beloved friends, or the train of events by which we are reduced from wealth to penury. No one, for instance, who has escaped from a shipwreck, from the brink of a precipice, from the jaws of a tiger, spends his days and nights in reviving his terrors past, re-imagining dangers not to occur again, or, if they do occur, from which the experience undergone can suggest no additional safeguards. The current of our life, indeed, like that of the rivers, is most rapid in the midmost channel, where all streams are alike comparatively slow in the depth and along the shores in which each life, as each river, has a character peculiar to itself. And hence, those who would sail with the tide of the world, as those who sail with the tide of a river, hasten to take the middle of the stream, as those who sail against the tide are found clinging to the shore. I returned to my habitual duties and avocations with renewed energy; I did not suffer my thoughts to dwell on the dreary wonders that had haunted me, from the evening I first met Sir Philip Derval to the morning on which I had quitted the house of his heir; whether realities or hallucinations, no guess of mine could unravel such marvels, and no prudence of mine guard me against their repetition. But I had no fear that they would be repeated, any more than the man who had gone through shipwreck, or the hairbreadth escape from a fall down a glacier, fears again to be found in a similar peril. Margrave had departed, whither I knew not, and, with his departure, ceased all sense of his influence. A certain calm within me, a tranquillizing feeling of relief, seemed to me like a pledge of permanent delivery.

But that which did accompany and haunt me, through all my occupations and pursuits, was the melancholy remembrance of the love I had lost in Lilian. I heard from Mrs. Ashleigh, who still frequently visited me, that her daughter seemed much in the same quiet state of mind,—perfectly reconciled to our separation, seldom mentioning my name, if mentioning it, with indifference; the only thing remarkable in her state was her aversion to all society, and a kind of lethargy that would come over her, often in the daytime. She would suddenly fall into sleep and so remain for hours, but a sleep that seemed very serene and tranquil, and from which she woke of herself. She kept much within her own room, and always retired to it when visitors were announced.

Mrs. Ashleigh began reluctantly to relinquish the persuasion she had so long and so obstinately maintained, that this state of feeling towards myself—and, indeed, this general change in Lilian—was but temporary and abnormal; she began to allow that it was best to drop all thoughts of a renewed engagement,—a future union. I proposed to see Lilian in her presence and in my professional capacity; perhaps some physical cause, especially for this lethargy, might be detected and removed. Mrs. Ashleigh owned to me that the idea had occurred to herself: she had sounded Lilian upon it: but her daughter had so resolutely opposed it,—had said with so quiet a firmness "that all being over between us, a visit from me would be unwelcome and painful,"—that Mrs. Ashleigh felt that an interview thus deprecated would only confirm estrangement. One day, in calling, she asked my advice whether it would not be better to try the effect of change of air and scene, and, in some other place, some other medical opinion might be taken? I approved of this suggestion with unspeakable sadness.

"And," said Mrs. Ashleigh, shedding tears, "if that experiment prove unsuccessful, I will write and let you know; and we must then consider what to say to the world as a reason why the marriage is broken off. I can render this more easy by staying away. I will not return to L— — till the matter has ceased to be the topic of talk, and at a distance any excuse will be less questioned and seem more natural. But still—still—let us hope still."

"Have you one ground for hope?"

"Perhaps so; but you will think it very frail and fallacious."

"Name it, and let me judge."

"One night—in which you were on a visit to Derval Court—"

"Ay, that night."

"Lilian woke me by a loud cry (she sleeps in the next room to me, and the door was left open); I hastened to her bedside in alarm; she was asleep, but appeared extremely agitated and convulsed. She kept calling on your name in a tone of passionate fondness, but as if in great terror. She cried, 'Do not go, Allen—do not go—you know not what you brave!—what you do!' Then she rose in her bed, clasping her hands. Her face was set and rigid; I tried to awake her, but could not. After a little time, she breathed a deep sigh, and murmured, 'Allen, Allen! dear love! did you not hear, did you not see me? What could thus baffle matter and traverse space but love and soul? Can you still doubt me, Allen?—doubt that I love you now, shall love you evermore?—yonder, yonder, as here below?' She then sank back on her pillow, weeping, and then I woke her."

"And what did she say on waking?"

"She did not remember what she had dreamed, except that she had passed through some great terror; but added, with a vague smile, 'It is over, and I feel happy now.' Then she turned round and fell asleep again, but quietly as a child, the tears dried, the smile resting."

"Go, my dear friend, go; take Lilian away from this place as soon
as you can; divert her mind with fresh scenes. I hope!—I do hope!
Let me know where you fix yourself. I will seize a holiday,—I need
one; I will arrange as to my patients; I will come to the same place;
she need not know of it, but I must be by to watch, to hear your
news of her. Heaven bless you for what you have said! I hope!—I do
hope!"

CHAPTER LIV.

Some days after, I received a few lines from Mrs. Ashleigh. Her arrangements for departure were made. They were to start the next morning. She had fixed on going into the north of Devonshire, and staying some weeks either at Ilfracombe or Lynton, whichever place Lilian preferred. She would write as soon as they were settled.

I was up at my usual early hour the next morning. I resolved to go out towards Mrs. Ashleigh's house, and watch, unnoticed, where I might, perhaps, catch a glimpse of Lilian as the carriage that would convey her to the railway passed my hiding-place.

I was looking impatiently at the clock; it was yet two hours before the train by which Mrs. Ashleigh proposed to leave. A loud ring at my bell! I opened the door. Mrs. Ashleigh rushed in, falling on my breast.

"Lilian! Lilian!"

"Heavens! What has happened?"

"She has left! she is gone,—gone away! Oh, Allen, how?—whither? Advise me. What is to be done?"

"Come in—compose yourself—tell me all,—clearly, quickly. Lilian gone,—gone away? Impossible! She must be hid somewhere in the house,—the garden; she, perhaps, did not like the journey. She may have crept away to some young friend's house. But I talk when you should talk: tell me all."

Little enough to tell! Lilian had seemed unusually cheerful the night before, and pleased at the thought of the excursion. Mother and daughter retired to rest early: Mrs. Ashleigh saw Lilian sleeping quietly before she herself went to bed. She woke betimes in the morning, dressed herself, went into the next room to call Lilian— Lilian was not there. No suspicion of flight occurred to her. Perhaps her daughter might be up already, and gone downstairs, remembering something she might wish to pack and take with her on the journey. Mrs. Ashleigh was confirmed in this idea when she noticed that her own room door was left open. She went downstairs, met a maidservant in the hall, who told her, with alarm and surprise, that both the street and garden doors were found unclosed. No one had seen Lilian. Mrs. Ashleigh now became seriously uneasy. On re-mounting to her daughter's room, she missed Lilian's bonnet and mantle. The house and garden were both searched in vain. There could be no doubt that Lilian had gone,—must have stolen noise-lessly at night through her mother's room, and let herself out of the house and through the garden.

"Do you think she could have received any letter, any message, any visitor unknown to you?"

"I cannot think it. Why do you ask? Oh, Allen, you do not believe there is any accomplice in this disappearance! No, you do not be-lieve it. But my child's honour! What will the world think?"

Not for the world cared I at that moment. I could think only of Lilian, and without one suspicion that imputed blame to her.

"Be quiet, be silent; perhaps she has gone on some visit and will return.
Meanwhile, leave inquiry to me."

CHAPTER LV.

It seemed incredible that Lilian could wander far without being observed. I soon ascertained that she had not gone away by the railway—by any public conveyance—had hired no carriage; she must therefore be still in the town, or have left it on foot. The greater part of the day was consumed in unsuccessful inquiries, and faint hopes that she would return; meanwhile the news of her disappearance had spread: how could such news fail to do so?

An acquaintance of mine met me under the archway of Monks' Gate. He wrung my hand and looked at me with great compassion.

"I fear," said he, "that we were all deceived in that young Margrave. He seemed so well conducted, in spite of his lively manners. But—"

"But what?"

"Mrs. Ashleigh was, perhaps, imprudent to admit him into her house so familiarly. He was certainly very handsome. Young ladies will be romantic."

"How dare you, sir!" I cried, choked with rage. "And without any colouring to so calumnious a suggestion! Margrave has not been in the town for many days. No one knows even where he is."

"Oh, yes, it is known where he is. He wrote to order the effects which he had left here to be sent to Penrith."

"When?"

"The letter arrived the day before yesterday. I happened to be calling at the house where he last lodged, when at L— —, the house opposite Mrs. Ashleigh's garden. No doubt the servants in both houses gossip with each other. Miss Ashleigh could scarcely fail to hear of Mr. Margrave's address from her maid; and since servants will exchange gossip, they may also convey letters. Pardon me, you know I am your friend."

"Not from the moment you breathe a word against my betrothed wife," said
I, fiercely.

I wrenched myself from the clasp of the man's hand, but his words still rang in my ears. I mounted my horse; I rode into the adjoining suburbs, the neighbouring villages; there, however, I learned nothing, till, just at nightfall, in a hamlet about ten miles from L——, a labourer declared he had seen a young lady dressed as I described, who passed by him in a path through the fields a little before noon; that he was surprised to see one so young, so well dressed, and a stranger to the neighbourhood (for he knew by sight the ladies of the few families scattered around) walking alone; that as he stepped out of the path to make way for her, he looked hard fnto her face, and she did not heed him,—seemed to gaze right before her, into space. If her expression had been less quiet and gentle, he should have thought, he could scarcely say why, that she was not quite right in her mind; there was a strange unconscious stare in her eyes, as if she were walking in her sleep. Her pace was very steady,—neither quick nor slow. He had watched her till she passed out of sight, amidst a wood through which the path wound its way to a village at some distance.

I followed up this clew. I arrived at the village to which my informant directed me, but night had set in. Most of the houses were closed, so I could glean no further information from the cottages or at the inn. But the police superintendent of the district lived in the village, and to him I gave instructions which I had not given, and, indeed, would have been disinclined to give, to the police at L——. He was intelligent and kindly; he promised to communicate at once with the different police-stations for miles round, and with all delicacy and privacy. It was not probable that Lilian could have wandered in one day much farther than the place at which I then was; it was scarcely to be conceived that she could baffle my pursuit and the practised skill of the police. I rested but a few hours, at a small public-house, and was on horseback again at dawn. A little after sunrise I again heard of the wanderer. At a lonely cottage, by a brick-kiln, in the midst of a wide common, she had stopped the previous evening, and asked for a draught of milk. The woman who gave it to her inquired if she had lost her way. She said "No;" and, only tarrying a few minutes, had gone across the common; and the woman supposed she was a visitor at a gentleman's house which was at the farther end of the waste, for the path she took led to no town, no village. It occurred to me then that Lilian avoided all high-roads, all places, even the humblest, where men congregated to-gether. But where could she have passed the night? Not to fatigue the reader with the fruitless result of frequent inquiries, I will but say that at the end of the second day I had succeeded in ascertaining that I was still on her track; and though I had ridden to and fro nearly double the distance—coming back again to places I had left behind—it was at the distance of forty miles from L—— that I last heard of her that second day. She had been sitting alone by a little brook only an hour before. I was led to the very spot by a wood-man—it was at the hour of twilight when he beheld her; she was leaning her face on her hand, and seemed weary. He spoke to her; she did not answer, but rose and resumed her way along the banks of the streamlet. That night I put up at no inn; I followed the course of the brook for miles, then struck into every path that I could con-ceive her to have taken,—in vain. Thus I consumed the night on foot, tying my horse to a tree, for he was tired out, and returning to him at sunrise. At noon, the third day, I again heard of her, and in a remote, savage part of the country. The features of the landscape were changed; there was little foliage and little culture, but the ground was broken into moulds and hollows, and covered with patches of heath and stunted brushwood. She had been seen by a shepherd, and he made the same observation as the first who had guided me on her track,—she looked to him "like some one walking in her sleep." An hour or two later, in a dell, amongst the furze-bushes, I chanced on a knot of ribbon. I recognized the colour Lilian habitually wore; I felt certain that the ribbon was hers. Calculating the utmost speed I could ascribe to her, she could not be far off, yet still I failed to discover her. The scene now was as solitary as a de-sert. I met no one on my way. At length, a little after sunset, I found myself in view of the sea. A small town nestled below the cliffs, on which I was guiding my weary horse. I entered the town, and while my horse was baiting went in search of the resident policeman. The information I had directed to be sent round the country had reached him; he had acted on it, but without result. I was surprised to hear

him address me by name, and looking at him more narrowly, I recognized him for the policeman Waby. This young man had always
expressed so grateful a sense of my attendance on his sister, and
had, indeed, so notably evinced his gratitude in prosecuting with
Margrave the inquiries which terminated in the discovery of Sir
Philip Derval's murderer, that I confided to him the name of the
wanderer, of which he had not been previously informed; but
which it would be, indeed, impossible to conceal from him should
the search in which his aid was asked prove successful,—as he
knew Miss Ashleigh by sight. His face immediately became
thoughtful. He paused a minute or two, and then said,—

"I think I have it, but I do not like to say; I may pain you, sir."

"Not by confidence; you pain me by concealment."

The man hesitated still: I encouraged him, and then he spoke out
frankly.

"Sir, did you never think it strange that Mr. Margrave should
move from his handsome rooms in the hotel to a somewhat uncom-
fortable lodging, from the window of which he could look down on
Mrs. Ashleigh's garden? I have seen him at night in the balcony of
that window, and when I noticed him going so frequently into Mrs.
Ashleigh's house during your unjust detention, I own, sir, I felt for
you—"

"Nonsense! Mr. Margrave went to Mrs. Ashleigh's house as my
friend. He has left L— — weeks ago. What has all this to do with—"

"Patience, sir; hear me out. I was sent from L— — to this station
(on promotion, sir) a fortnight since last Friday, for there has been a
good deal of crime hereabouts; it is a bad neighbourhood, and full
of smugglers. Some days ago, in watching quietly near a lonely
house, of which the owner is a suspicious character down in my
books, I saw, to my amazement, Mr. Margrave come out of that
house,—come out of a private door in it, which belongs to a part of
the building not inhabited by the owner, but which used formerly,
when the house was a sort of inn, to be let to night lodgers of the
humblest description. I followed him; he went down to the seashore, walked about, singing to himself; then returned to the house,
and re-entered by the same door. I soon learned that he lodged in

the house,—had lodged there for several days. The next morning, a fine yacht arrived at a tolerably convenient creek about a mile from the house, and there anchored. Sailors came ashore, rambling down to this town. The yacht belonged to Mr. Margrave; he had purchased it by commission in London. It is stored for a long voyage. He had directed it to come to him in this out-of-the-way place, where no gentleman's yacht ever put in before, though the creek or bay is handy enough for such craft. Well, sir, is it not strange that a rich young gentleman should come to this unfrequented seashore, put up with accommodation that must be of the rudest kind, in the house of a man known as a desperate smuggler, suspected to be worse; order a yacht to meet him here; is not all this strange? But would it be strange if he were waiting for a young lady? And if a young lady has fled at night from her home, and has come secretly along bypaths, which must have been very fully explained to her beforehand, and is now near that young gentleman's lodging, if not actually in it—if this be so, why, the affair is not so very strange after all. And now do you forgive me, sir?"

"Where is this house? Lead me to it."

"You can hardly get to it except on foot; rough walking, sir, and about seven miles off by the shortest cut."

"Come, and at once; come quickly. We must be there before— before—"

"Before the young lady can get to the place. Well, from what you say of the spot in which she was last seen, I think, on reflection, we may easily do that. I am at your service, sir. But I should warn you that the owners of the house, man and wife, are both of villanous character,—would do anything for money. Mr. Margrave, no doubt, has money enough; and if the young lady chooses to go away with Mr. Margrave, you know I have no power to help it."

"Leave all that to me; all I ask of you is to show me the house."

We were soon out of the town; the night had closed in; it was very dark, in spite of a few stars; the path was rugged and precipitous, sometimes skirting the very brink of perilous cliffs, sometimes delving down to the seashore—there stopped by rock or wave—and painfully rewinding up the ascent.

"It is an ugly path, sir, but it saves four miles; and anyhow the road is a bad one."

We came, at last, to a few wretched fishermen's huts. The moon had now risen, and revealed the squalor of poverty-stricken ruinous hovels; a couple of boats moored to the shore, a moaning, fretful sea; and at a distance a vessel, with lights on board, lying perfectly still at anchor in a sheltered curve of the bold rude shore. The policeman pointed to the vessel.

"The yacht, sir; the wind will be in her favour if she sails tonight."

We quickened our pace as well as the nature of the path would permit, left the huts behind us, and about a mile farther on came to a solitary house, larger than, from the policeman's description of Margrave's lodgement, I should have presupposed: a house that in the wilder parts of Scotland might be almost a laird's; but even in the moonlight it looked very dilapidated and desolate. Most of the windows were closed, some with panes broken, stuffed with wisps of straw; there were the remains of a wall round the house; it was broken in some parts (only its foundation left). On approaching the house I observed two doors,—one on the side fronting the sea, one on the other side, facing a patch of broken ground that might once have been a garden, and lay waste within the enclosure of the ruined wall, encumbered with various litter; heaps of rubbish, a ruined shed, the carcass of a worn-out boat. This latter door stood wide open,—the other was closed. The house was still and dark, as if either deserted, or all within it retired to rest.

"I think that open door leads at once to the rooms Mr. Margrave hires; he can go in and out without disturbing the other inmates. They used to keep, on the side which they inhabit, a beer-house, but the magistrates shut it up; still, it is a resort for bad characters. Now, sir, what shall we do?

"Watch separately. You wait within the enclosure of the wall, hid by those heaps of rubbish, near the door; none can enter but what you will observe them. If you see her, you will accost and stop her, and call aloud for me; I shall be in hearing. I will go back to the high part of the ground yonder—it seems to me that she must pass that way; and I would desire, if possible, to save her from the humiliation, the—the shame of coming within the precincts of that man's abode. I feel I may trust you now and hereafter. It is a great thing for the happiness and honour of this poor young lady and her mother, that I may be able to declare that I did not take her from that man, from any man—from that house, from any house. You comprehend me, and will obey? I speak to you as a confidant,—a friend."

"I thank you with my whole heart, sir, for so doing. You saved my sister's life, and the least I can do is to keep secret all that would pain your life if blabbed abroad. I know what mischief folks' tongues can make. I will wait by the door, never fear, and will rather lose my place than not strain all the legal power I possess to keep the young lady back from sorrow."

This dialogue was interchanged in close hurried whisper behind the broken wall, and out of all hearing. Waby now crept through a wide gap into the inclosure, and nestled himself silently amidst the wrecks of the broken boat, not six feet from the open door, and close to the wall of the house itself. I went back some thirty yards up the road, to the rising ground which I had pointed out to him. According to the best calculation I could make—considering the pace at which I had cleared the precipitous pathway, and reckoning from the place and time at which Lilian had been last seen-she could not possibly have yet entered that house. I might presume it would be more than half an hour before she could arrive; I was in hopes that, during the interval, Margrave might show himself, perhaps at the door, or from the windows, or I might even by some light from the latter be guided to the room in which to find him. If, after waiting a reasonable time, Lilian should fail to appear, I had formed my plan of action; but it was important for the success of that plan that I should not lose myself in the strange house, nor bring its owners to Margrave's aid,—that I should surprise him alone and unawares. Half an hour, three quarters, a whole hour thus passed. No sign of my poor wanderer; but signs there were of the enemy from whom I resolved, at whatever risk, to free and to save her. A window on the ground-floor, to the left of the door, which had long fixed my attention because I had seen light through the chinks of the shutters, slowly unclosed, the shutters fell back, the casement opened, and I beheld Margrave distinctly; he held something in his hand that gleamed in the moonlight, directed not towards the mound on which I stood, nor towards the path I had taken, but towards an open space beyond the ruined wall to the right. Hid by a cluster of stunted shrubs I watched him with a heart that beat with rage, not with terror. He seemed so intent in his own gaze as to be unheeding or unconscious of all else. I stole from my post, and, still under cover, sometimes of the broken wall, sometimes of the shaggy ridges that skirted the path, crept on, on till I reached the side of the house itself; then, there secure from his eyes, should he turn them, I stepped over the ruined wall, scarcely two feet high in that place, on—on towards the door. I passed the spot on which the policeman had shrouded himself; he was seated, his back against the ribs of the broken boat. I put my hand to his mouth that he might not cry out in surprise, and whispered in his ear; he stirred not. I shook him by the arm: still he stirred not. A ray of the moon fell on his face. I saw that he was in a profound slumber. Persuaded that it was no natural sleep, and that he had become useless to me, I passed him by. I was at the threshold of the open door, the light from the window close by falling on the ground; I was in the passage; a glimmer came through the chinks of a door to the left; I turned the handle noiselessly, and, the next moment, Margrave was locked in my grasp.

"Call out," I hissed in his ear, "and I strangle you before any one can come to your help."

He did not call out; his eye, fixed on mine as he writhed round, saw, perhaps, his peril if he did. His countenance betrayed fear, but as I tightened my grasp that expression gave way to one of wrath and fierceness; and as, in turn, I felt the grip of his hand, I knew that the struggle between us would be that of two strong men, each equally bent on the mastery of the other.

I was, as I have said before, endowed with an unusual degree of physical power, disciplined in early youth by athletic exercise and contest. In height and in muscle I had greatly the advantage over my antagonist; but such was the nervous vigour, the elastic energy of his incomparable frame, in which sinews seemed springs of steel, that had our encounter been one in which my strength was less heightened by rage, I believe that I could no more have coped with him than the bison can cope with the boa; but I was animated by that passion which trebles for a time all our forces,—which makes even the weak man a match for the strong. I felt that if I were worsted, disabled, stricken down, Lilian might be lost in losing her sole protector; and on the other hand, Margrave had been taken at the disadvantage of that surprise which will half unnerve the fiercest of the wild beasts; while as we grappled, reeling and rocking to and fro in our struggle, I soon observed that his attention was distracted,—that his eye was turned towards an object which he had dropped involuntarily when I first seized him. He sought to drag me towards that object, and when near it stooped to seize. It was a bright, slender, short wand of steel. I remembered when and where I had seen it, whether in my waking state or in vision; and as his hand stole down to take it from the floor, I set on the wand my strong foot. I cannot tell by what rapid process of thought and association I came to the belief that the possession of a little piece of blunted steel would decide the conflict in favor of the possessor; but the struggle now was concentred on the attainment of that seemingly idle weapon. I was becoming breathless and exhausted, while Margrave seemed every moment to gather up new force, when collecting all my strength for one final effort, I lifted him suddenly high in the air, and hurled him to the farthest end of the cramped arena to which our contest was confined. He fell, and with a force by which most men would have been stunned; but he recovered himself with a quick rebound, and, as he stood facing me, there was something grand as well as terrible in his aspect. His eyes literally flamed, as those of a tiger; his rich hair, flung back from his knitted forehead, seemed to erect itself as an angry mane; his lips, slightly parted, showed the glitter of his set teeth; his whole frame seemed larger in the tension of the muscles, and as, gradually relaxing his first defying and haughty attitude, he crouched as the panther crouches for its deadly spring, I felt as if it were a wild beast, whose rush was coming upon me,—wild beast, but still Man, the king of the animals, fashioned forth from no mixture of humbler races by the slow revolutions of time, but his royalty stamped on his form when the earth became fit for his coming.[1]

At that moment I snatched up the wand, directed it towards him, and advancing with a fearless stride, cried,—

"Down to my feet, miserable sorcerer!"

To my own amaze, the effect was instantaneous. My terrible antagonist dropped to the floor as a dog drops at the word of his master. The muscles of his frowning countenance relaxed, the glare of his wrathful eyes grew dull and rayless; his limbs lay prostrate and unnerved, his head rested against the wall, his arms limp and drooping by his side. I approached him slowly and cautiously; he seemed cast into a profound slumber.

"You are at my mercy now!" said I.

He moved his head as in sign of deprecating submission.

"You hear and understand me? Speak!"

His lips faintly muttered, "Yes."

"I command you to answer truly the questions I shall address to you."

"I must, while yet sensible of the power that has passed to your hand."

"Is it by some occult magnetic property in this wand that you have exercised so demoniac an influence over a creature so pure as Lilian Ashleigh?"

"By that wand and by other arts which you could not comprehend."

"And for what infamous object,—her seduction, her dishonour?"

"No! I sought in her the aid of a gift which would cease did she cease to be pure. At first I but cast my influence upon her that through her I might influence yourself. I needed your help to discover a secret. Circumstances steeled your mind against me. I could no longer hope that you would voluntarily lend yourself to my will. Meanwhile, I had found in her the light of a loftier knowledge than that of your science; through that knowledge, duly heeded and cultivated, I hoped to divine what I cannot of myself discover. Therefore I deepened over her mind the spells I command; therefore I have drawn her hither as the loadstone draws the steel, and therefore I would have borne her with me to the shores to which I was about this night to sail. I had cast the inmates of the house and all around it into slumber, in order that none might witness her departure; had I not done so, I should have summoned others to my aid, in spite of your threat."

"And would Lilian Ashleigh have passively accompanied you, to her own irretrievable disgrace?"

"She could not have helped it; she would have been unconscious of her acts; she was, and is, in a trance; nor, had she gone with me, would she have waked from that state while she lived; that would not have been long."

"Wretch! and for what object of unhallowed curiosity do you exert an influence which withers away the life of its victim?"

"Not curiosity, but the instinct of self-preservation. I count on no life beyond the grave. I would defy the grave, and live on."

"And was it to learn, through some ghastly agencies, the secret of renewing existence, that you lured me by the shadow of your own image on the night when we met last?"

The voice of Margrave here became very faint as he answered me, and his countenance began to exhibit the signs of an exhaustion almost mortal.

"Be quick," he murmured, "or I die. The fluid which emanates from that wand, in the hand of one who envenoms that fluid with his own hatred and rage, will prove fatal to my life. Lower the wand from my forehead! low — low, — lower still!"

"What was the nature of that rite in which you constrained me to share?"

"I cannot say. You are killing me. Enough that you were saved from a great danger by the apparition of the protecting image vouchsafed to your eye; otherwise you would — you would — Oh, release me! Away! away!"

The foam gathered to his lips; his limbs became fearfully convulsed.

"One question more: where is Lilian at this moment? Answer that question, and I depart."

He raised his head, made a visible effort to rally his strength, and gasped out, —

"Yonder. Pass through the open space up the cliff, beside a thorn-tree; you will find her there, where she halted when the wand dropped from my hand. But—but—beware! Ha! you will serve me yet, and through her! They said so that night, though you heard them not. They said it!" Here his face became death-like; he pressed his hand on his heart, and shrieked out, "Away! away! or you are my murderer!"

I retreated to the other end of the room, turning the wand from him, and when I gained the door, looked back; his convulsions had ceased, but he seemed locked in a profound swoon.

I left the room,—the house,—paused by Waby; he was still sleeping. "Awake!" I said, and touched him with the wand. He started up at once, rubbed his eyes, began stammering out excuses. I checked them, and bade him follow me. I took the way up the open ground towards which Margrave had pointed the wand, and there, motionless, beside a gnarled fantastic thorn-tree, stood Lilian. Her arms were folded across her breast; her face, seen by the moonlight, looked so innocent and so infantine, that I needed no other evidence to tell me how unconscious she was of the peril to which her steps had been drawn. I took her gently by the hand. "Come with me," I said in a whisper, and she obeyed me silently, and with a placid smile.

Rough though the way, she seemed unconscious of fatigue. I placed her arm in mine, but she did not lean on it. We got back to the town. I obtained there an old chaise and a pair of horses. At morning Lilian was under her mother's roof. About the noon of that day fever seized her; she became rapidly worse, and, to all appearance, in imminent danger. Delirium set in; I watched beside her night and day, supported by an inward conviction of her recovery, but tortured by the sight of her sufferings. On the third day a change for the better became visible; her sleep was calm, her breathing regular.

Shortly afterwards she woke out of danger. Her eyes fell at once on me, with all their old ineffable tender sweetness.

"Oh, Allen, beloved, have I not been very ill? But I am almost well now. Do not weep; I shall live for you,—for your sake." And she bent forward, drawing my hand from my streaming eyes, and kissed me with a child's guileless kiss on my burning forehead.

[1] And yet, even if we entirely omit the consideration of the soul, that immaterial and immortal principle which is for a time united to his body, and view him only in his merely animal character, man is still the most excellent of animals. — Dr. Kidd, On the Adaptation of External Nature to the Physical Condition of Man (Sect. iii. p. 18).

CHAPTER LVI.

Lilian recovered, but the strange thing was this: all memory of the weeks that had elapsed since her return from visiting her aunt was completely obliterated; she seemed in profound ignorance of the charge on which I had been confined,—perfectly ignorant even of the existence of Margrave. She had, indeed, a very vague reminiscence of her conversation with me in the garden,—the first conversation which had ever been embittered by a disagreement,—but that disagreement itself she did not recollect. Her belief was that she had been ill and light-headed since that evening. From that evening to the hour of her waking, conscious and revived, all was a blank. Her love for me was restored, as if its thread had never been broken. Some such instances of oblivion after bodily illness or mental shock are familiar enough to the practice of all medical men;[1] and I was therefore enabled to appease the anxiety and wonder of Mrs. Ashleigh, by quoting various examples of loss, or suspension, of memory. We agreed that it would be necessary to break to Lilian, though very cautiously, the story of Sir Philip Derval's murder, and the charge to which I had been subjected. She could not fail to hear of those events from others. How shall I express her womanly terror, her loving, sympathizing pity, on hearing the tale, which I softened as well as I could?

"And to think that I knew nothing of this!" she cried, clasping my hand; "to think that you were in peril, and that I was not by your side!"

Her mother spoke of Margrave, as a visitor,—an agreeable, lively stranger; Lilian could not even recollect his name, but she seemed shocked to think that any visitor had been admitted while I was in circumstances so awful! Need I say that our engagement was renewed? Renewed! To her knowledge and to her heart it had never been interrupted for a moment. But oh! the malignity of the wrong world! Oh, that strange lust of mangling reputations, which seizes on hearts the least wantonly cruel! Let two idle tongues utter a tale against some third person, who never offended the babblers, and how the tale spreads, like fire, lighted none know how, in the herbage of an American prairie! Who shall put it out?

What right have we to pry into the secrets of other men's hearths? True or false, the tale that is gabbled to us, what concern of ours can it be? I speak not of cases to which the law has been summoned, which law has sifted, on which law has pronounced. But how, when the law is silent, can we assume its verdicts? How be all judges where there has been no witness-box, no cross-examination, no jury? Yet, every day we put on our ermine, and make ourselves judges,—judges sure to condemn, and on what evidence? That which no court of law will receive. Somebody has said something to somebody, which somebody repeats to everybody!

The gossip of L—— had set in full current against Lilian's fair name. No ladies had called or sent to congratulate Mrs. Ashleigh on her return, or to inquire after Lilian herself during her struggle between life and death.

How I missed the Queen of the Hill at this critical moment! How I longed for aid to crush the slander, with which I knew not how to grapple,—aid in her knowledge of the world and her ascendancy over its judgments! I had heard from her once since her absence, briefly but kindly expressing her amazement at the ineffable stupidity which could for a moment have subjected me to a suspicion of Sir Philip Derval's strange murder, and congratulating me heartily on my complete vindication from so monstrous a charge. To this letter no address was given. I supposed the omission to be accidental, but on calling at her house to inquire her direction, I found that the servants did not know it.

What, then, was my joy when just at this juncture I received a note from Mrs. Poyntz, stating that she had returned the night before, and would be glad to see me.

I hastened to her house. "Ah," thought I, as I sprang lightly up the ascent to the Hill, "how the tattlers will be silenced by a word from her imperial lips!" And only just as I approached her door did it strike me how difficult—nay, how impossible—to explain to her—the hard positive woman, her who had, less ostensibly but more ruthlessly than myself, destroyed Dr. Lloyd for his belief in the comparatively rational pretensions of clairvoyance—all the mystical excuses for Lilian's flight from her home? How speak to her — or, indeed, to any one — about an occult fascination and a magic wand? No matter: surely it would be enough to say that at the time Lilian had been light-headed, under the influence of the fever which had afterwards nearly proved fatal, The early friend of Anne Ashleigh would not be a severe critic on any tale that might right the good name of Anne Ashleigh's daughter. So assured, with a light heart and a cheerful face, I followed the servant into the great lady's pleasant but decorous presence-chamber.

[1] Such instances of suspense of memory are recorded in most physiological and in some metaphysical works. Dr. Abercrombie notices some, more or less similar to that related in the text: "A young lady who was present at a catastrophe in Scotland, in which many people lost their lives by the fall of the gallery of a church, escaped without any injury, but with the complete loss of the recollection of any of the circumstances; and this extended not only to the accident, but to everything that had occurred to her for a certain time before going to church. A lady whom I attended some years ago in a protracted illness, in which her memory became much impaired, lost the recollection of a period of about ten or twelve years, but spoke with perfect consistency of things as they stood before that time." Dr. Aberercmbie adds: "As far as I have been able to trace it, the principle in such cases seems to be, that when the memory is impaired to a certain degree, the loss of it extends backward to some event or some period by which a particularly deep impression had been made upon the mind." — ABERCROMBIE: On the Intellectual Powers, pp. 118, 119 (15th edition).

CHAPTER LVII.

Mrs. Poyntz was on her favourite seat by the window, and for a wonder, not knitting—that classic task seemed done; but she was smoothing and folding the completed work with her white comely hand, and smiling over it, as if in complacent approval, when I entered the room. At the fire-side sat the he-colonel inspecting a newly-invented barometer; at another window, in the farthest recess of the room, stood Miss Jane Poyntz, with a young gentleman whom I had never before seen, but who turned his eyes full upon me with a haughty look as the servant announced my name. He was tall, well proportioned, decidedly handsome, but with that expression of cold and concentred self-esteem in his very attitude, as well as his countenance, which makes a man of merit unpopular, a man without merit ridiculous.

The he-colonel, always punctiliously civil, rose from his seat, shook hands with me cordially, and said, "Coldish weather to-day; but we shall have rain to-morrow. Rainy seasons come in cycles. We are about to commence a cycle of them with heavy showers." He sighed, and returned to his barometer.

Miss Jane bowed to me graciously enough, but was evidently a little confused,—a circumstance which might well attract my notice, for I had never before seen that high-bred young lady deviate a hairsbreadth from the even tenor of a manner admirable for a cheerful and courteous ease, which, one felt convinced, would be unaltered to those around her if an earthquake swallowed one up an inch before her feet.

The young gentleman continued to eye me loftily, as the heir-apparent to some celestial planet might eye an inferior creature from a half-formed nebula suddenly dropped upon his sublime and perfected, star.

Mrs. Poyntz extended to me two fingers, and said frigidly, "Delighted to see you again! How kind to attend so soon to my note!"

Motioning me to a seat beside her, she here turned to her husband, and said, "Poyntz, since a cycle of rain begins tomorrow, better secure your ride to-day. Take these young people with you. I want to talk with Dr. Fenwick."

The colonel carefully put away his barometer, and saying to his daughter, "Come!" went forth. Jane followed her father; the young gentleman followed Jane.

The reception I had met chilled and disappointed me. I felt that Mrs. Poyntz was changed, and in her change the whole house seemed changed. The very chairs looked civilly unfriendly, as if preparing to turn their backs on me. However, I was not in the false position of an intruder; I had been summoned; it was for Mrs. Poyntz to speak first, and I waited quietly for her to do so.

She finished the careful folding of her work, and then laid it at rest in the drawer of the table at which she sat. Having so done, she turned to me, and said,—

"By the way, I ought to have introduced to you my young guest, Mr. Ashleigh Sumner. You would like him. He has talents,—not showy, but solid. He will succeed in public life."

"So that young man is Mr. Ashleigh Sumner? I do not wonder that Miss
Ashleigh rejected him."

I said this, for I was nettled, as well as surprised, at the coolness with which a lady who had professed a friendship for me mentioned that fortunate young gentleman, with so complete an oblivion of all the antecedents that had once made his name painful to my ear.

In turn, my answer seemed to nettle Mrs. Poyntz.

"I am not so sure that she did reject; perhaps she rather misunderstood him; gallant compliments are not always proposals of marriage. However that be, his spirits were not much damped by Miss Ashleigh's disdain, nor his heart deeply smitten by her charms; for he is now very happy, very much attached to another young lady, to whom he proposed three days ago, at Lady Delafield's, and not to make a mystery of what all our little world will know before tomorrow, that young lady is my daughter Jane."

"Were I acquainted with Mr. Sumner, I should offer to him my sincere congratulations."

Mrs. Poyntz resumed, without heeding a reply more complimentary to Miss
Jane than to the object of her choice, —

"I told you that I meant Jane to marry a rich country gentleman, and Ashleigh Sumner is the very country gentleman I had then in my thoughts. He is cleverer and more ambitious than I could have hoped; he will be a minister some day, in right of his talents, and a peer, if he wishes it, in right of his lands. So that matter is settled."

There was a pause, during which my mind passed rapidly through links of reminiscence and reasoning, which led me to a mingled sentiment of admiration for Mrs. Poyntz as a diplomatist and of distrust for Mrs. Poyntz as a friend. It was now clear why Mrs. Poyntz, before so little disposed to approve my love, had urged me at once to offer my hand to Lilian, in order that she might depart affianced and engaged to the house in which she would meet Mr. Ashleigh Sumner. Hence Mrs. Poyntz's anxiety to obtain all the information I could afford her of the sayings and doings at Lady Haughton's; hence, the publicity she had so suddenly given to my engagement; hence, when Mr. Sumner had gone away a rejected suitor, her own departure from L— —; she had seized the very moment when a vain and proud man, piqued by the mortification received from one lady, falls the easier prey to the arts which allure his suit to another. All was so far clear to me. And I—was my self-conceit less egregious and less readily duped than that of yon glided popinjay's! How skilfully this woman had knitted me into her work with the noiseless turn of her white hands! and yet, forsooth, I must vaunt the superior scope of my intellect, and plumb all the fountains of Nature,—I, who could not fathom the little pool of this female schemer's mind!

But that was no time for resentment to her or rebuke to myself. She was now the woman who could best protect and save from slander my innocent, beloved Lilian. But how approach that perplexing subject?

Mrs. Poyntz approached it, and with her usual decision of purpose, which bore so deceitful a likeness to candour of mind.

"But it was not to talk of my affairs that I asked you to call, Allen Fenwick." As she uttered my name, her voice softened, and her manner took that maternal, caressing tenderness which had sometimes amused and sometimes misled me. "No, I do not forget that you asked me to be your friend, and I take without scruple the license of friendship. What are these stories that I have heard already about Lilian Ashleigh, to whom you were once engaged?"

"To whom I am still engaged."

"Is it possible? Oh, then, of course the stories I have heard are all false. Very likely; no fiction in scandal ever surprises me. Poor dear Lilian, then, never ran away from her mother's house?"

I smothered the angry pain which this mode of questioning caused me; I knew how important it was to Lilian to secure to her the countenance and support of this absolute autocrat; I spoke of Lilian's long previous distemper of mind; I accounted for it as any intelligent physician, unacquainted with all that I could not reveal, would account. Heaven forgive me for the venial falsehood, but I spoke of the terrible charge against myself as enough to unhinge for a time the intellect of a girl so acutely sensitive as Lilian; I sought to create that impression as to the origin of all that might otherwise seem strange; and in this state of cerebral excitement she had wandered from home—but alone. I had tracked every step of her way; I had found and restored her to her home. A critical delirium had followed, from which she now rose, cured in health, unsuspicious that there could be a whisper against her name. And then, with all the eloquence I could command, and in words as adapted as I could frame them to soften the heart of a woman, herself a mother, I implored Mrs. Poyntz's aid to silence all the cruelties of calumny, and extend her shield over the child of her own early friend.

When I came to an end, I had taken, with caressing force, Mrs. Poyntz's reluctant hands in mine. There were tears in my voice, tears in my eyes. And the sound of her voice in reply gave me hope, for it was unusually gentle. She was evidently moved. The hope was soon quelled.

"Allen Fenwick," she said, "you have a noble heart; I grieve to see how it abuses your reason. I cannot aid Lilian Ashleigh in the way you ask. Do not start back so indignantly. Listen to me as patiently as I have listened to you. That when you brought back the unfortunate young woman to her poor mother, her mind was disordered, and became yet more dangerously so, I can well believe; that she is now recovered, and thinks with shame, or refuses to think at all, of her imprudent flight, I can believe also; but I do not believe, the World cannot believe, that she did not, knowingly and purposely, quit her mother's roof, and in quest of that young stranger so incautiously, so unfeelingly admitted to her mother's house during the very time you were detained on the most awful of human accusations. Every one in the town knows that Mr. Margrave visited daily at Mrs. Ashleigh's during that painful period; every one in the town knows in what strange out-of-the-way place this young man had niched himself; and that a yacht was bought, and lying in wait there. What for? It is said that the chaise in which you brought Miss Ashleigh back to her home was hired in a village within an easy reach of Mr. Margrave's lodging—of Mr. Margrave's yacht. I rejoice that you saved the poor girl from ruin; but her good name is tarnished; and if Anne Ashleigh, whom I sincerely pity, asks me my advice, I can but give her this: 'Leave L——, take your daughter abroad; and if she is not to marry Mr. Margrave, marry her as quietly and as quickly as possible to some foreigner.'"

"Madam! madam! this, then, is your friendship to her—to me! Oh, shame on you to insult thus an affianced husband! Shame on me ever to have thought you had a heart!"

"A heart, man!" she exclaimed, almost fiercely, springing up, and startling me with the change in her countenance and voice. "And little you would have valued, and pitilessly have crushed this heart, if I had suffered myself to show it to you! What right have you to reproach me? I felt a warm interest in your career, an unusual attraction in your conversation and society. Do you blame me for that, or should I blame myself? Condemned to live amongst brainless puppets, my dull occupation to pull the strings that moved them, it was a new charm to my life to establish friendship and intercourse with intellect and spirit and courage. Ah! I understand that look, half incredulous, half inquisitive."

"Inquisitive, no; incredulous, yes! You desired my friendship, and how does your harsh judgment of my betrothed wife prove either to me or to her mother, whom you have known from your girlhood, the first duty of a friend,—which is surely not that of leaving a friend's side the moment that he needs countenance in calumny, succour in trouble!"

"It is a better duty to prevent the calumny and avert the trouble. Leave aside Anne Ashleigh, a cipher that I can add or abstract from my sum of life as I please. What is my duty to yourself? It is plain. It is to tell you that your honour commands you to abandon all thoughts of Lilian Ashleigh as your wife. Ungrateful that you are! Do you suppose it was no mortification to my pride of woman and friend, that you never approached me in confidence except to ask my good offices in promoting your courtship to another; no shock to the quiet plans I had formed as to our familiar though harmless intimacy, to hear that you were bent on a marriage in which my friend would be lost to me?"

"Not lost! not lost! On the contrary, the regard I must suppose you had for Lilian would have been a new link between our homes."

"Pooh! Between me and that dreamy girl there could have been no sympathy, there could have grown up no regard. You would have been chained to your fireside, and—and—but no matter. I stifled my disappointment as soon as I felt it,—stifled it, as all my life I have stifled that which either destiny or duty—duty to myself as to others—forbids me to indulge. Ah, do not fancy me one of the weak criminals who can suffer a worthy liking to grow into a debasing love! I was not in love with you, Allen Fenwick."

"Do you think I was ever so presumptuous a coxcomb as to fancy it?"

"No," she said, more softly; "I was not so false to my household ties and to my own nature. But there are some friendships which are as jealous as love. I could have cheerfully aided you in any choice which my sense could have approved for you as wise; I should have been pleased to have found in such a wife my most intimate companion. But that silly child!—absurd! Nevertheless, the freshness and enthusiasm of your love touched me; you asked my aid, and I gave it. Perhaps I did believe that when you saw more of Lilian Ashleigh you would be cured of a fancy conceived by the eye—I should have known better what dupes the wisest men can be to the witcheries of a fair face and eighteen! When I found your illusion obstinate, I wrenched myself away from a vain regret, turned to my own schemes and my own ambition, and smiled bitterly to think that, in pressing you to propose so hastily to Lilian, I made your blind passion an agent in my own plans. Enough of this. I speak thus openly and boldly to you now, because now I have not a sentiment that can interfere with the dispassionate soundness of my counsels. I repeat, you cannot now marry Lilian Ashleigh; I cannot take my daughter to visit her; I cannot destroy the social laws that I myself have set in my petty kingdom."

"Be it as you will. I have pleaded for her while she is still Lilian Ashleigh. I plead for no one to whom I have once given my name. Before the woman whom I have taken from the altar, I can place, as a shield sufficient, my strong breast of man. Who has so deep an interest in Lilian's purity as I have? Who is so fitted to know the exact truth of every whisper against her? Yet when I, whom you admit to have some reputation for shrewd intelligence,—I, who tracked her way,—I, who restored her to her home,—when I, Allen Fenwick, am so assured of her inviolable innocence in thought as in deed, that I trust my honour to her keeping,—surely, surely, I confute the scandal which you yourself do not believe, though you refuse to reject and to annul it?"

"Do not deceive yourself, Allen Fenwick," said she, still standing beside me, her countenance now hard and stern. "Look where I stand, I am the World! The World, not as satirists depreciate, or as optimists extol its immutable properties, its all-persuasive authority. I am the World! And my voice is the World's voice when it thus warns you. Should you make this marriage, your dignity of character and position would be gone! If you look only to lucre and professional success, possibly they may not ultimately suffer. You have skill, which men need; their need may still draw patients to your door and pour guineas into your purse. But you have the pride, as well as the birth of a gentleman, and the wounds to that pride will be hourly chafed and never healed. Your strong breast of man has no shelter to the frail name of woman. The World, in its health, will look down on your wife, though its sick may look up to you. This is not all. The World, in its gentlest mood of indulgence, will say compassionately, 'Poor man! how weak, and how deceived! What an unfortunate marriage!' But the World is not often indulgent,—it looks most to the motives most seen on the surface. And the World will more frequently say, 'No; much too clever a man to be duped! Miss Ashleigh had money. A good match to the man who liked gold better than honour.'"

I sprang to my feet, with difficulty suppressing my rage; and, remembering it was a woman who spoke to me, "Farewell, madam," said I, through my grinded teeth. "Were you, indeed, the Personation of The World, whose mean notions you mouth so calmly, I could not disdain you more." I turned to the door, and left her still standing erect and menacing, the hard sneer on her resolute lip, the red glitter in her remorseless eye.

CHAPTER LVIII.

If ever my heart vowed itself to Lilian, the vow was now the most trustful and the most sacred. I had relinquished our engagement before; but then her affection seemed, no matter from what cause; so estranged from me, that though I might be miserable to lose her, I deemed that she would be unhappy in our union. Then, too, she was the gem and darling of the little world in which she lived; no whisper assailed her: now I knew that she loved me; I knew that her estrangement had been involuntary; I knew that appearances wronged her, and that they never could be explained. I was in the true position of man to woman: I was the shield, the bulwark, the fearless confiding protector! Resign her now because the world babbled, because my career might be impeded, because my good name might be impeached, — resign her, and, in that resignation, confirm all that was said against her! Could I do so, I should be the most craven of gentlemen, the meanest of men!

I went to Mrs. Ashleigh, and entreated her to hasten my union with her daughter, and fix the marriage-day.

I found the poor lady dejected and distressed. She was now sufficiently relieved from the absorbing anxiety for Lilian to be aware of the change on the face of that World which the woman I had just quitted personified and concentred; she had learned the cause from the bloodless lips of Miss Brabazon.

"My child! my poor child!" murmured the mother. "And she so guileless, — so sensitive! Could she know what is said, it would kill her. She would never marry you, Allen, — she would never bring shame to you!"

"She never need learn the barbarous calumny. Give her to me, and at once; patients, fortune, fame, are not found only at L— —. Give her to me at once. But let me name a condition: I have a patrimonial independence, I have amassed large savings, I have my profession and my repute. I cannot touch her fortune — I cannot, — never can! Take it while you live; when you die, leave it to accumu-

late for her children, if children she have; not to me; not to her—
unless I am dead or ruined!"

"Oh, Allen, what a heart! what a heart! No, not heart, Allen,—that
bird in its cage has a heart: soul—what a soul!"

CHAPTER LIX.

How innocent was Lilian's virgin blush when I knelt to her, and prayed that she would forestall the date that had been fixed for our union, and be my bride before the breath of the autumn had withered the pomp of thewoodland and silenced the song of the birds! Meanwhile, I was so fearfully anxious that she should risk no danger of hearing, even of surmising, the cruel slander against her—should meet no cold contemptuous looks, above all, should be safe from the barbed talk of Mrs. Poyntz—that I insisted on the necessity of immediate change of air and scene. I proposed that we should all three depart, the next day, for the banks of my own beloved and native Windermere. By that pure mountain air, Lilian's health would be soon re-established; in the church hallowed to me by the graves of my fathers our vows should be plighted. No calumny had ever cast a shadow over those graves. I felt as if my bride would be safer in the neighbourhood of my mother's tomb.

I carried my point: it was so arranged. Mrs. Ashleigh, however, was reluctant to leave before she had seen her dear friend, Margaret Poyntz. I had not the courage to tell her what she might expect to hear from that dear friend, but, as delicately as I could, I informed her that I had already seen the Queen of the Hill, and contradicted the gossip that had reached her; but that as yet, like other absolute sovereigns, the Queen of the Hill thought it politic to go with the popular stream, reserving all check on its direction till the rush of its torrent might slacken; and that it would be infinitely wiser in Mrs. Ashleigh to postpone conversation with Mrs. Poyntz until Lilian's return to L— — as my wife. Slander by that time would have wearied itself out, and Mrs. Poyntz (assuming her friendship to Mrs. Ashleigh to be sincere) would then be enabled to say with authority to her subjects, "Dr. Fenwick alone knows the facts of the story, and his marriage with Miss Ashleigh refutes all the gossip to her prejudice."

I made that evening arrangements with a young and rising practitioner to secure attendance on my patients during my absence. I passed the greater part of the night in drawing up memoranda to guide my proxy in each case, however humble the sufferer. This task finished, I chanced, in searching for a small microscope, the wonders of which I thought might interest and amuse Lilian, to open a drawer in which I kept the manuscript of my cherished Physiological Work, and, in so doing, my eye fell upon the wand which I had taken from Margrave. I had thrown it into that drawer on my return home, after restoring Lilian to her mother's house, and, in the anxiety which had subsequently preyed upon my mind, had almost forgotten the strange possession I had as strangely acquired. There it now lay, the instrument of agencies over the mechanism of nature which no doctrine admitted by my philosophy could accept, side by side with the presumptuous work which had analyzed the springs by which Nature is moved, and decided the principles by which reason metes out, from the inch of its knowledge, the plan of the Infinite Unknown.

I took up the wand and examined it curiously. It was evidently the work of an age far remote from our own, scored over with half-obliterated characters in some Eastern tongue, perhaps no longer extant. I found that it was hollow within. A more accurate observation showed, in the centre of this hollow, an exceedingly fine thread-like wire, the unattached end of which would slightly touch the palm when the wand was taken into the hand. Was it possible that there might be a natural and even a simple cause for the effects which this instrument produced? Could it serve to collect, from that great focus of animal heat and nervous energy which is placed in the palm of the human hand, some such latent fluid as that which Reichenbach calls the "odic," and which, according to him, "rushes through and pervades universal Nature"? After all, why not? For how many centuries lay unknown all the virtues of the loadstone and the amber? It is but as yesterday that the forces of vapour have become to men genii more powerful than those conjured up by Aladdin; that light, at a touch, springs forth from invisible air; that thought finds a messenger swifter than the wings of the fabled Afrite. As, thus musing, my hand closed over the wand, I felt a wild thrill through my frame. I recoiled; I was alarmed lest (according to the plain common-sense theory of Julius Faber) I might be preparing my imagination to form and to credit its own illusions. Hastily I laid down the wand. But then it occurred to me that whatever its properties, it had so served the purposes of the dread Fascinator from whom it had been taken, that he might probably seek to repossess himself of it; he might contrive to enter my house in my absence; more prudent to guard in my own watchful keeping the incomprehensible instrument of incomprehensible arts. I resolved, therefore, to take the wand with me, and placed it in my travelling-trunk, with such effects as I selected for use in the excursion that was to commence with the morrow. I now lay down to rest, but I could not sleep. The recollections of the painful interview with Mrs. Poyntz became vivid and haunting. It was clear that the sentiment she had conceived for me was that of no simple friendship,—something more or something less, but certainly something else; and this conviction brought before me that proud hard face, disturbed by a pang wrestled against but not subdued, and that clear metallic voice, troubled by the quiver of an emotion which, perhaps, she had never analyzed to herself. I did not need her own assurance to know that this sentiment was not to be confounded with a love which she would have despised as a weakness and repelled as a crime; it was an inclination of the intellect, not a passion of the heart. But still it admitted a jealousy little less keen than that which has love for its cause,—so true it is that jealousy is never absent where self-love is always present. Certainly, it was no susceptibility of sober friendship which had made the stern arbitress of a coterie ascribe to her interest in me her pitiless judgment of Lilian. Strangely enough, with the image of this archetype of conventional usages and the trite social life, came that of the mysterious Margrave, surrounded by all the attributes with which superstition clothes the being of the shadowy border-land that lies beyond the chart of our visual world itself. By what link were creatures so dissimilar riveted together in the metaphysical chain of association? Both had entered into the record of my life when my life admitted its own first romance of love. Through the aid of this cynical schemer I had been made known to Lilian. At her house I had heard the dark story of that Louis Grayle, with whom, in mocking spite of my reason, conjectures, which that very reason must depose itself before it could resolve into distempered fancies, identified the enigmatical Margrave. And now both she, the representative of the formal world most opposed to visionary creeds, and he, who gathered round him all the terrors which haunt the realm of fable, stood united against me,—foes with whom the intellect I had so haughtily cultured knew not how to cope. Whatever assault I might expect from either, I was unable to assail again. Alike, then, in this, are the Slander and the Phantom,—that which appalls us most in their power over us is our impotence against them.

But up rose the sun, chasing the shadows from the earth, and brightening insensibly the thoughts of man. After all, Margrave had been baffled and defeated, whatever the arts he had practised and the secrets he possessed. It was, at least, doubtful whether his evil machinations would be renewed. He had seemed so incapable of long-sustained fixity of purpose, that it was probable he was already in pursuit of some new agent or victim; and as to this commonplace and conventional spectre, the so-called World, if it is everywhere to him whom it awes, it is nowhere to him who despises it. What was the good or bad word of a Mrs. Poyntz to me? Ay, but to Lilian? There, indeed, I trembled; but still, even in trembling, it was sweet to think that my home would be her shelter,—my choice her vindication. Ah! how unutterably tender and reverential Love becomes when it assumes the duties of the guardian, and hallows its own heart into a sanctuary of refuge for the beloved!

CHAPTER LX.

The beautiful lake! We two are on its grassy margin, — twilight melting into night; the stars stealing forth, one after one. What a wonderful change is made within us when we come from our callings amongst men, chafed, wearied, wounded; gnawed by our cares, perplexed by the doubts of our very wisdom, stung by the adder that dwells in cities, — Slander; nay, even if renowned, fatigued with the burden of the very names that we have won! What a change is made within us when suddenly we find ourselves transported into the calm solitudes of Nature, — into scenes familiar to our happy dreaming childhood; back, back from the dusty thoroughfares of our toil-worn manhood to the golden fountain of our youth! Blessed is the change, even when we have no companion beside us to whom the heart can whisper its sense of relief and joy. But if the one in whom all our future is garnered up be with us there, instead of that weary World which has so magically vanished away from the eye and the thought, then does the change make one of those rare epochs of life in which the charm is the stillness. In the pause from all by which our own turbulent struggles for happiness trouble existence, we feel with a rapt amazement how calm a thing it is to be happy. And so as the night, in deepening, brightened, Lilian and I wandered by the starry lake. Conscious of no evil in ourselves, how secure we felt from evil! A few days more — a few days more, and we two should be as one! And that thought we uttered in many forms of words, brooding over it in the long intervals of enamoured silence.

And when we turned back to the quiet inn at which we had taken up our abode, and her mother, with her soft face, advanced to meet us, I said to Lilian, —

"Would that in these scenes we could fix our home for life, away and afar from the dull town we have left behind us, with the fret of its wearying cares and the jar of its idle babble!"

"And why not, Allen? Why not? But no, you would not be happy."

"Not be happy, and with you? Sceptic, by what reasoning do you arrive at that ungracious conclusion?"

"The heart loves repose and the soul contemplation, but the mind needs action. Is it not so?"

"Where learned you that aphorism, out of place on such rosy lips?"

"I learned it in studying you," murmured Lilian, tenderly.

Here Mrs. Ashleigh joined us. For the first time I slept under the same roof as Lilian. And I forgot that the universe contained an enigma to solve or an enemy to fear.

CHAPTER LXI.

Twenty days — the happiest my life had ever known — thus glided on. Apart from the charm which love bestows on the beloved, there was that in Lilian's conversation which made her a delightful companion. Whether it was that, in this pause from the toils of my career, my mind could more pliantly supple itself to her graceful imagination, or that her imagination was less vague and dreamy amidst those rural scenes, which realized in their loveliness and grandeur its long-conceived ideals, than it had been in the petty garden-ground neighboured by the stir and hubbub of the busy town, — in much that I had once slighted or contemned as the vagaries of undisciplined fancy, I now recognized the sparkle and play of an intuitive genius, lighting up many a depth obscure to instructed thought. It is with some characters as with the subtler and more ethereal order of poets, — to appreciate them we must suspend the course of artificial life; in the city we call them dreamers, on the mountain-top we find them interpreters.

In Lilian, the sympathy with Nature was not, as in Margrave, from the joyous sense of Nature's lavish vitality; it was refined into exquisite perception of the diviner spirit by which that vitality is informed. Thus, like the artist, from outward forms of beauty she drew forth the covert types, lending to things the most familiar exquisite meanings unconceived before. For it is truly said by a wise critic of old, that "the attribute of Art is to suggest infinitely more than it expresses; "and such suggestions, passing from the artist's innermost thought into the mind that receives them, open on and on into the Infinite of Ideas, as a moonlit wave struck by a passing oar impels wave upon wave along one track of light.

So the days glided by, and brought the eve of our bridal morn. It had been settled that, after the ceremony (which was to be performed by license in the village church, at no great distance, which adjoined my paternal home, now passed away to strangers), we should make a short excursion into Scotland, leaving Mrs. Ashleigh to await our return at the little inn.

I had retired to my own room to answer some letters from anxious patients, and having finished these I looked into my trunk for a Guide-Book to the North, which I had brought with me. My hand came upon Margrave's wand, and remembering that strange thrill which had passed through me when I last handled it, I drew it forth, resolved to examine calmly if I could detect the cause of the sensation. It was not now the time of night in which the imagination is most liable to credulous impressions, nor was I now in the anxious and jaded state of mind in which such impressions may be the more readily conceived. The sun was slowly setting over the delicious landscape; the air cool and serene; my thoughts collected, — heart and conscience alike at peace. I took, then, the wand, and adjusted it to the palm of the hand as I had done before. I felt the slight touch of the delicate wire within, and again the thrill! I did not this time recoil; I continued to grasp the wand, and sought deliberately to analyze my own sensations in the contact. There came over me an increased consciousness of vital power; a certain exhilaration, elasticity, vigour, such as a strong cordial may produce on a fainting man. All the forces of my frame seemed refreshed, redoubled; and as such effects on the physical system are ordinarily accompanied by correspondent effects on the mind, so I was sensible of a proud elation of spirits, — a kind of defying, superb self-glorying. All fear seemed blotted out from my thought, as a weakness impossible to the grandeur and might which belong to Intellectual Man; I felt as if it were a royal delight to scorn Earth and its opinions, brave Hades and its spectres. Rapidly this new-born arrogance enlarged itself into desires vague but daring. My mind reverted to the wild phenomena associated with its memories of Margrave. I said half-aloud, "if a creature so beneath myself in constancy of will and completion of thought can wrest from Nature favours so marvellous, what could not be won from her by me, her patient persevering seeker? What if there be spirits around and about, invisible to the common eye, but whom we can submit to our control; and what if this rod be charged with some occult fluid, that runs through all creation, and can be so disciplined as to establish communication wherever life and thought can reach to beings that live and think? So would the mystics of old explain what perplexes me. Am I sure that the mystics of old duped them selves or their pupils? This, then, this slight wand, light as a reed in my grasp, this, then, was the instrument by which Margrave sent his irresistible will through air and space, and by which I smote himself, in the midst of his tiger-like wrath, into the helplessness of a sick man's swoon! Can the instrument at this distance still control him; if now meditating evil, disarm and disable his purpose?" Involuntarily, as I revolved these ideas, I stretched forth the wand, with a concentred energy of desire that its influence should reach Margrave and command him. And since I knew not his whereabout, yet was vaguely aware that, according to any conceivable theory by which the wand could be supposed to carry its imagined virtues to definite goals in distant space, it should be pointed in the direction of the object it was in-tended to affect, so I slowly moved the wand as if describing a cir-cle; and thus, in some point of the circle—east, west, north, or south—the direction could not fail to be true. Before I had per-formed half the circle, the wand of itself stopped, resisting palpably the movement of my hand to impel it onward. Had it, then, found the point to which my will was guiding it, obeying my will by some magnetic sympathy never yet comprehended by any recognized science? I know not; but I had not held it thus fixed for many se-conds, before a cold air, well remembered, passed by me, stirring the roots of my hair; and, reflected against the opposite wall, stood the hateful Scin-Laeca. The Shadow was dimmer in its light than when before beheld, and the outline of the features was less distinct; still it was the unmistakable lemur, or image, of Margrave.

And a voice was conveyed to my senses, saying, as from a great distance, and in weary yet angry accents,

"You have summoned me? Wherefore?"

I overcame the startled shudder with which, at first, I beheld the Shadow and heard the Voice.

"I summoned you not," said I; "I sought but to impose upon you my will, that you should persecute, with your ghastly influences, me and mine no more. And now, by whatever authority this wand bestows on me, I so abjure and command you!"

I thought there was a sneer of disdain on the lip through which the answer seemed to come,—

"Vain and ignorant, it is but a shadow you command. My body you have cast into a sleep, and it knows not that the shadow is here; nor, when it wakes, will the brain be aware of one reminiscence of the words that you utter or the words that you hear."

"What, then, is this shadow that simulates the body? Is it that which in popular language is called the soul?"

"It is not: soul is no shadow."

"What then?"

"Ask not me. Use the wand to invoke Intelligences higher than mine."

"And how?"

"I will tell you not. Of yourself you may learn, if you guide the wand by your own pride of will and desire; but in the hands of him who has learned not the art, the wand has its dangers. Again I say you have summoned me! Wherefore?"

"Lying shade, I summoned thee not."

"So wouldst thou say to the demons, did they come in their terrible wrath, when the bungler, who knows not the springs that he moves, calls them up unawares, and can neither control nor dispel. Less revengeful than they, I leave thee unharmed, and depart."

"Stay. If, as thou sayest, no command I address to thee — to thee, who art only the image or shadow — can have effect on the body and mind of the being whose likeness thou art, still thou canst tell me what passes now in his brain. Does it now harbour schemes against me through the woman I love? Answer truly."

"I reply for the sleeper, of whom I am more than a likeness, though only the shadow. His thought speaks thus: 'I know, Allen Fenwick, that in thee is the agent I need for achieving the end that I seek. Through the woman thou lovest, I hope to subject thee. A grief that will harrow thy heart is at hand; when that grief shall befall, thou wilt welcome my coming. In me alone thy hope will be placed; through me alone wilt thou seek a path out of thy sorrow. I shall ask my conditions: they will make thee my tool and my slave!'"

The shadow waned,—it was gone. I did not seek to detain it, nor, had I sought, could I have known by what process. But a new idea now possessed me. This shadow, then, that had once so appalled and controlled me, was, by its own confession, nothing more than a shadow! It had spoken of higher Intelligences; from them I might learn what the Shadow could not reveal. As I still held the wand firmer and firmer in my grasp, my thoughts grew haughtier and bolder. Could the wand, then, bring those loftier beings thus darkly referred to before me? With that thought, intense and engrossing, I guided the wand towards the space, opening boundless and blue from the casement that let in the skies. The wand no longer resisted my hand.

In a few moments I felt the floors of the room vibrate; the air was darkened; a vaporous, hazy cloud seemed to rise from the ground without the casement; an awe, infinitely more deep and solemn than that which the Scin-Laeca had caused in its earliest apparition, curdled through my veins, and stilled the very beat of my heart.

At that moment I heard, without, the voice of Lilian, singing a simple, sacred song which I had learned at my mother's knees, and taught to her the day before: singing low, and as with a warning angel's voice. By an irresistible impulse I dashed the wand to the ground, and bowed my head as I had bowed it when my infant mind comprehended, without an effort, mysteries more solemn than those which perplexed me now. Slowly I raised my eyes, and looked round; the vaporous, hazy cloud had passed away, or melted into the ambient rose-tints amidst which the sun had sunk.

Then, by one of those common reactions from a period of overstrained excitement, there succeeded to that sentiment of arrogance and daring with which these wild, half-conscious invocations had been fostered and sustained, a profound humility, a warning fear.

"What!" said I, inly, "have all those sound resolutions, which my reason founded on the wise talk of Julius Faber, melted away in the wrack of haggard, dissolving fancies! Is this my boasted intellect, my vaunted science! I—I, Allen Fenwick, not only the credulous believer, but the blundering practitioner, of an evil magic! Grant what may be possible, however uncomprehended,—grant that in this accursed instrument of antique superstition there be some real powers—chemical, magnetic, no matter what-by which the imagination can be aroused, inflamed, deluded, so that it shapes the things I have seen, speaks in the tones I have heard,—grant this, shall I keep ever ready, at the caprice of will, a constant tempter to steal away my reason and fool my senses? Or if, on the other hand, I force my sense to admit what all sober men must reject; if I un-school myself to believe that in what I have just experienced there is no mental illusion; that sorcery is a fact, and a demon world has gates which open to a key that a mortal can forge,—who but a saint would not shrink from the practice of powers by which each passing thought of ill might find in a fiend its abettor? In either case—in any case—while I keep this direful relic of obsolete arts, I am haunted,—cheated out of my senses, unfitted for the uses of life. If, as my ear or my fancy informs me, grief—human grief—is about to befall me, shall I, in the sting of impatient sorrow, have recourse to an aid which, the same voice declares, will reduce me to a tool and a slave,—tool and slave to a being I dread as a foe? Out on these nightmares! and away with the thing that bewitches the brain to conceive them!"

I rose; I took up the wand, holding it so that its hollow should not rest on the palm of the hand. I stole from the house by the back way, in order to avoid Lilian, whose voice I still heard, singing low, on the lawn in front. I came to a creek, to the bank of which a boat was moored, undid its chain, rowed on to a deep part of the lake, and dropped the wand into its waves. It sank at once; scarcely a ripple furrowed the surface, not a bubble arose from the deep. And, as the boat glided on, the star mirrored itself on the spot where the placid waters had closed over the tempter to evil.

Light at heart, I sprang again on the shore, and hastening to Lilian, where she stood on the silvered, shining sward, clasped her to my breast.

"Spirit of my life!" I murmured, "no enchantments for me but thine! Thine are the spells by which creation is beautified, and, in that beauty, hallowed. What though we can see not into the measureless future from the verge of the moment; what though sorrow may smite us while we are dreaming of bliss, let the future not rob me of thee, and a balm will be found for each wound! Love me ever as now, oh, my Lilian; troth to troth, side by side, till the grave!"

"And beyond the grave," answered Lilian, softly.

CHAPTER LXII.

Our vows are exchanged at the altar, the rite which made Lilian my wife is performed; we are returned from the church amongst the hills, in which my fathers had worshipped; the joy-bells that had pealed for my birth had rung for my marriage. Lilian has gone to her room to prepare for our bridal excursion; while the carriage we have hired is waiting at the door. I am detaining her mother on the lawn, seeking to cheer and compose her spirits, painfully affected by that sense of change in the relations of child and parent which makes itself suddenly felt by the parent's heart on the day that secures to the child another heart on which to lean.

But Mrs. Ashleigh's was one of those gentle womanly natures which, if easily afflicted, are easily consoled. And, already smiling through her tears, she was about to quit me and join her daughter, when one of the inn-servants came to me with some letters, which had just been delivered by the postman. As I took them from the servant, Mrs. Ashleigh asked if there were any for her. She expected one from her housekeeper at L— —, who had been taken ill in her absence, and about whom the kind mistress felt anxious. The servant replied that there was no letter for her, but one directed to Miss Ashleigh, which he had just sent up to the young lady.

Mrs. Ashleigh did not doubt that her housekeeper had written to Lilian, whom she had known from the cradle and to whom she was tenderly attached, instead of to her mistress; and, saying something to me to that effect, quickened her steps towards the house.

I was glancing over my own letters, chiefly from patients, with a rapid eye, when a cry of agony, a cry as if of one suddenly stricken to the heart, pierced my ear,—a cry from within the house. "Heavens! was that Lilian's voice?" The same doubt struck Mrs. Ashleigh, who had already gained the door. She rushed on, disappearing within the threshold and calling to me to follow. I bounded forward, passed her on the stairs, was in Lilian's room before her.

My bride was on the floor prostrate, insensible: so still, so colour-less, that my first dreadful thought was that life had gone. In her hand was a letter, crushed as with a convulsive sudden grasp.

It was long before the colour came back to her cheek, before the breath was perceptible on her lip. She woke, but not to health, not to sense. Hours were passed in violent convulsions, in which I momentarily feared her death. To these succeeded stupor, lethargy, not benignant sleep. That night, my bridal night, I passed as in some chamber to which I had been summoned to save youth from the grave. At length—at length—life was rescued, was assured! Life came back, but the mind was gone. She knew me not, nor her mother. She spoke little and faintly; in the words she uttered there was no reason.

I pass hurriedly on; my experience here was in fault, my skill ineffectual. Day followed day, and no ray came back to the darkened brain. We bore her, by gentle stages, to London. I was sanguine of good result from skill more consummate than mine, and more especially devoted to diseases of the mind. I summoned the first advisers. In vain! in vain!

CHAPTER LXIII.

And the cause of this direful shock? Not this time could it be traced to some evil spell, some phantasmal influence. The cause was clear, and might have produced effects as sinister on nerves of stronger fibre if accompanied by a heart as delicately sensitive, an honour as exquisitely pure.

The letter found in her hand was without name; it was dated from L— —, and bore the postmark of that town. It conveyed to Lilian, in the biting words which female malice can make so sharp, the tale we had sought sedulously to guard from her ear,—her flight, the construction that scandal put upon it. It affected for my blind infatuation a contemptuous pity; it asked her to pause before she brought on the name I offered to her an indelible disgrace. If she so decided, she was warned not to return to L— —, or to prepare there for the sentence that would exclude her from the society of her own sex. I cannot repeat more, I cannot minute down all that the letter expressed or implied, to wither the orange blossoms in a bride's wreath. The heart that took in the venom cast its poison on the brain, and the mind fled before the presence of a thought so deadly to all the ideas which its innocence had heretofore conceived.

I knew not whom to suspect of the malignity of this mean and miserable outrage, nor did I much care to know. The handwriting, though evidently disguised, was that of a woman, and, therefore, had I discovered the author, my manhood would have forbidden me the idle solace of revenge. Mrs. Poyntz, however resolute and pitiless her hostility when once aroused, was not without a certain largeness of nature irreconcilable with the most dastardly of all the weapons that envy or hatred can supply to the vile. She had too lofty a self-esteem and too decorous a regard for the moral sentiment of the world that she typified, to do, or connive at, an act which degrades the gentlewoman. Putting her aside, what other female enemy had Lilian provoked? No matter! What other woman at L— — was worth the condescension of a conjecture?

After listening to all that the ablest of my professional brethren in the metropolis could suggest to guide me, and trying in vain their remedies, I brought back my charge to L— —. Retaining my former residence for the visits of patients, I engaged, for the privacy of my home, a house two miles from the town, secluded in its own grounds, and guarded by high walls.

Lilian's mother removed to my mournful dwelling-place. Abbot's House, in the centre of that tattling coterie, had become distasteful to her, and to me it was associated with thoughts of anguish and of terror. I could not, without a shudder, have entered its grounds, — could not, without a stab at the heart, have seen again the old fairy-land round the Monks' Well, nor the dark cedar-tree under which Lilian's hand had been placed in mine; and a superstitious remembrance, banished while Lilian's angel face had brightened the fatal precincts, now revived in full force. The dying man's curse—had it not been fulfilled?

A new occupant for the old house was found within a week after Mrs. Ashleigh had written from London to a house-agent at L— —, intimating her desire to dispose of the lease. Shortly before we had gone to Windermere, Miss Brabazon had become enriched by a liberal life-annuity bequeathed to her by her uncle, Sir Phelim. Her means thus enabled her to move from the comparatively humble lodging she had hitherto occupied to Abbot's House; but just as she had there commenced a series of ostentatious entertainments, implying an ambitious desire to dispute with Mrs. Poyntz the sovereignty of the Hill, she was attacked by some severe malady which appeared complicated with spinal disease, and after my return to L— — I sometimes met her, on the spacious platform of the Hill, drawn along slowly in a Bath chair, her livid face peering forth from piles of Indian shawls and Siberian furs, and the gaunt figure of Dr. Jones stalking by her side, taciturn and gloomy as some sincere mourner who conducts to the grave the patron on whose life he himself had conveniently lived. It was in the dismal month of February that I returned to L— —, and I took possession of my plighted nuptial home on the anniversary of the very day in which I had passed through the dead dumb world from the naturalist's gloomy death-room.